9011

745.594
COR   Corwin, Judith
           Hoffman

           Easter crafts

DUE DATE	BRODART	05/99	5.95

Easter Crafts

Easter Crafts

★ A Holiday Craft Book ★

★ Judith Hoffman Corwin ★

FRANKLIN WATTS

New York ★ Chicago ★ London ★ Toronto ★ Sydney

★ **Also by Judith Hoffman Corwin** ★

African Crafts
Asian Crafts
Latin American and Caribbean Crafts

Colonial American Crafts: The Home
Colonial American Crafts: The School
Colonial American Crafts: The Village

Halloween Crafts
Valentine Crafts

Papercrafts

Forthcoming Books

Christmas Crafts
Hanukkah Crafts
Kwanzaa Crafts
Thanksgiving Crafts

★ **For Jules Arthur and Oliver Jamie** ★

Library of Congress Cataloging-in-Publication Data

Corwin, Judith Hoffman.
    Easter crafts / Judith Hoffman Corwin.
      p.   cm.—(Holiday crafts)
    Includes index.
    ISBN 0-531-11145-8
    1. Easter decorations—Juvenile literature.   2. Handicraft—
Juvenile literature.   3. Easter cookery—Juvenile literature.
[1. Easter decorations.   2. Handicraft.]   I. Title.
TT900.E2C667   1994
745.594′1—dc20   93-21258 CIP AC

Contents

About Easter

Easter is a joyful spring holiday. Bouquets of spring flowers, decorated Easter eggs, Easter baskets filled with jellybeans and chocolate eggs are all part of the fun. At Easter, we celebrate the earth's new year of growth, after the cold, dark days of winter. Eastre, the goddess of spring, gave the Easter festival its name and favorite animal, the rabbit. The rabbit, or hare, represents love, fertility, and growth. Many people around the world have a day to celebrate the arrival of spring.

Easter has its beginnings in ancient Christian holidays, pagan celebrations, and spring festivals. Long before the celebration of Easter, people celebrated a spring festival. The sun was an important part of the celebration. Without it, there would be no life on earth. The people feasted, danced, sang, and exchanged gifts. They rejoiced over the rebirth of life in the fields and forests. Today these customs and legends combine to make our Easter Sunday.

Easter is some time between March 22 and April 25 and comes at the end of the Christian Holy Week. It may fall on the first Sunday after the first full moon following March 21, which is the first day of spring.

The Easter egg is a good example of a custom that began many thousands of years ago. For ancient peoples, the symbol of new life was an egg. When the shell was broken, a new life came into the world. Some myths state that the world itself began in an huge egg. The world-egg split in two. The upper half became the heavens and the lower half the earth. For thousands of years, it has been a custom to give eggs as gifts during the spring festival. Today we have fun dyeing them in bright colors and decorating them with simple designs.

Other customs and practices of Easter include wearing new clothes to celebrate the new year of life. In New York City and many other big cities, an important part of the holiday is the Easter Parade. People stroll in their new clothes, with many women and young girls wearing Easter bonnets, hats that have been decorated with flowers and pretty ribbons.

Flowers are a popular gift at Easter, especially the Easter lily, which also decorates the churches. Other flowers typical of Easter are the daffodil, tulip, narcissus, and pussy willow.

Let's Get Started

This book tells you about the Easter holiday, its legends and its history and it is full of ideas for making greeting cards, decorations, gift wrappings, presents, and wonderful treats to eat. Often, you will be able to make everything yourself, using everyday household supplies and objects. Use your imagination and you will be surprised at what you can create. The treasures you make will add color and excitement to your holiday celebrations.

Directions for some of the projects include patterns for you to use to make a copy of what is shown. You don't want to cut up this book, so copy the pattern with tracing paper. Begin by placing a piece of tracing paper over the pattern in the book. Using a pencil with a soft lead, trace the outline of the pattern. Turn the paper over and rub all over the pattern with the pencil. Turn it over again, and tape or hold it down carefully on the paper or fabric you have chosen to work with. Draw over your original lines, pressing hard on the pencil. Lift the tracing-paper pattern and you are ready to go on with the other instructions for your project.★

Create Your Own Easter Cards

Here's a rabbit holding a carrot, a robin in its nest with three eggs, a sheep with a butterfly on its back, and a chick with an Easter egg. All of these cards are fun to make and are three-dimensional. A small piece of sponge added to the designs makes them especially interesting.

HERE'S WHAT YOU WILL NEED★

5″ × 6″ piece of oaktag for each card
scrap of oaktag
tracing paper, carbon paper, tape
pencil, scissors, glue
¼″ square piece of sponge for each card
black fine-line marker
colored markers or pencils

HERE'S HOW TO DO IT★

1. Choose which card you want to make and trace it on the tracing paper.

2. Place the 5″ × 6″ piece of oaktag on your table. Tape a piece of carbon paper to the oaktag. Now tape the traced design on top of the carbon paper. Draw over the original lines.

3. Remove the tracing paper and the carbon paper. Draw over the lines with the black marker. Color the design any way you like. Now repeat these steps on the scrap of oaktag for the three-dimensional part of your Easter card (the carrot, robin, butterfly, or chick). Cut it out.

4. Checking the illustration, glue the ¼″ square piece of sponge to the 5″ × 6″ Easter card. Glue the three-dimensional piece to the sponge. Write an Easter greeting on your card. ★

11

★   ★

Blowing Out an Egg

It's great fun to decorate Easter eggs and here's a way to keep them for a long time. You can empty out the eggshell by blowing out the insides.

HERE'S WHAT YOU WILL NEED★

raw eggs
long sharp needle
small bowl
paper towels
white glue

HERE'S HOW TO DO IT★

1. Hold the egg firmly but gently, and with the needle, pierce a hole in each end of the egg. Make one hole larger than the other.

2. Pass the needle through the larger hole and, breaking the yolk inside, stir the contents.

3. Blow into the small hole and force the egg out of the large hole into the small bowl. If you're planning to make cookies soon, you can use these blown-out eggs.

4. Clean out the shell by running a little water through the large hole. Gently shake the egg as you rinse until it is completely clean. If you don't do this, the eggs will begin to smell after a while. Let it dry on a paper towel.

5. After the shell has dried, you can put a few drops of glue over each hole to protect the egg from further cracking. Now it is ready to decorate. ★

Oliver the Baby Dragon in an Egg

Here's a real surprise—a baby dragon in an egg. You will need an egg that has been blown out, so follow the directions on page 15. Carefully crack the egg in half; you don't have to worry if some of it breaks into pieces. You will need only one half of the shell in one piece. Use the broken pieces to surround the egg after it has been glued to the base.

HERE'S WHAT YOU WILL NEED★

1 blown-out egg
4″ square of oaktag, for the base
scrap of white oaktag, for Oliver
black fine-line marker
red and green markers
white glue
tracing paper, pencil, tape
scissors

HERE'S HOW TO DO IT★

1.   Carefully break off the top half of the eggshell and crumble it into pieces, leaving the bottom half in one piece.

2.   Glue the half of the egg that's in one piece to the base, as shown in the illustration. Surround it with the leftover pieces of eggshell and glue them to the base, also.

3.   To make a pattern for Oliver, place the tracing paper over the design and draw over it with a pencil. Turn the paper over and with the point of a pencil, rub hard along the lines of the pattern on the back. Turn the paper over again and place it on the scrap of white oaktag. Tape it down to hold it while you draw over your original lines. Remove the tracing paper and tape.

4.   Draw over the pencil lines on the oaktag with the black marker. Color Oliver green, with red eyes and scales along his back. Glue the dragon to the eggshell, as shown in the illustration. ★

18

Design Your Own Easter Eggs

These two pages have many interesting designs. Choose the ones that you like best to use on your Easter eggs. The eggs should be hard-boiled, or you can blow them out, as described on page 15. Then draw the designs on the eggs with a permanent black fine-line marker. Color the eggs any way you like using felt-tip markers, or acrylic, or water-color paints. You can also try drawing the designs on the eggs with crayons and then dipping the eggs in a bowl of food coloring. The crayon designs will show through and make a beautiful egg.

Another decorating method is to draw the designs with colored felt-tip markers and then touch them up or give them some details such as dots, lines, and so on, with a gold metallic marker. You can also paint the eggs with clear nail polish to make them shiny after you have finished decorating them. Each one will be your own original work.

You can use the designs on pages 20 and 21 for Easter cards, gift wrapping paper, and T-shirt decorations. Follow the directions on page 9 and copy the designs onto your project. To decorate a T-shirt, be sure to use permanent felt-tip markers.

Easter Baskets

Pretty Easter baskets can be made from almost any small container that doesn't have printing on it and that will hold at least four eggs. A small white gift box, a green cardboard strawberry container, or a plastic tomato container will all work well. An empty straw basket that your mother lets you borrow would also be good.

HERE'S WHAT YOU WILL NEED★

small container
colored construction paper
scraps of fabric
buttons, beads
rickrack, ribbon, lace
white glue, tape, scissors

HERE'S HOW TO DO IT★

1. Pick a container to use for your Easter basket. Look at the illustrations on the opposite page to get some ideas on how you would like to decorate it. Use your imagination as you plan your design and glue on the fabric, buttons, beads, rickrack, ribbon, and lace.

2. Add to the decorations on your basket by cutting hearts out of pink or red construction paper and gluing them on. If you are working with a basket, instead of using glue, attach the hearts with a small piece of tape, rolled in a circle and stuck on the back of each heart.

3. You can cut daisies out of yellow construction paper and glue or tape them to the basket, too.

4. Tie bows on your basket with the ribbon. Yellow and purple are Easter colors.

5. Cut green construction paper into thin strips to make some "grass." Make as much grass as you need to fill up the bottom of the basket to make a nest for your decorated Easter eggs.

6. Your Easter basket is now all ready for the eggs that you have decorated and the jellybeans and other candy that you have collected.★

Jellybean Pouch

Jellybean sacks are great containers that are fun to decorate. They make good presents. They can also be put into your Easter basket. If you use a gold metallic marker to highlight the designs, they will really look sharp.

HERE'S WHAT YOU WILL NEED★

¼ yard muslin fabric
1 yard of ½" red ribbon
pencil, ruler, scissors
tracing paper, carbon paper, tape, white glue
black fine-line marker, colored markers
gold metallic marker, cardboard (optional)

HERE'S HOW TO DO IT★

1. For each jellybean pouch, cut a piece of muslin 4" wide by 8" long. Fold the fabric in half along the 8" side so that you have a 4" square. The edge opposite the folded edge is to be left open.

2. To form the pouch, open the muslin again and put a small amount of glue along the two outside edges. Close again and press to secure the sack.

3. Choose the designs you want to make and trace them onto the tracing paper.

4. Place a piece of carbon paper on the pouch and tape it down gently. Next tape the traced design on top of the carbon paper.

5. Draw over the design firmly with a pencil. Remove the tracing paper and carbon paper. Draw over the outline of the design with the black marker. Color in the rest of the design any way you like. If you are using the gold metallic marker, put a piece of cardboard inside the pouch so the marker won't go through the muslin. Add dots, stripes, stars, and any other designs that you like. Check the illustrations for some ideas.

6. Cut an 8" piece of ribbon for each of the pouches. Fill each sack with jellybeans to about an inch from the top. Tie the pouch with the ribbon and make a bow. Repeat this for each pouch. ★

Little White Rabbit

Here's a recipe for a flour-and-salt "clay" that is quick and easy to make. You can shape this little rabbit out of it. If you roll out the clay to a ¼" thickness, you can copy the pattern for the bunny cookies on page 43 and make "clay" rabbits that you can color with acrylic paints. All of these items would make wonderful additions to your Easter basket.

HERE'S WHAT YOU WILL NEED★

measuring cup
2 cups flour, 1 cup salt, 1 cup water, to make the "clay"
large mixing bowl, mixing spoon, rolling pin
knife, toothpick, yarn (optional)
cookie sheet, aluminum foil, potholder
black fine-line marker
white and red acrylic paints
brush
cardboard

HERE'S HOW TO DO IT★

1. Mix the flour and salt together in a large bowl. Then add the water a little at a time, mixing it in. When all the water is in, mix the dough well with your hands. This is called kneading.

2. If you are making a rabbit like the cookies on page 43, make the pattern for it now. Then put some extra flour on a clean working surface and, with the rolling pin, roll the dough to about ¼" thickness.

3. Place the cardboard pattern on the dough. Hold the cardboard down with one hand, and using a knife, carefully cut around the pattern. If you like, use a toothpick to make a hole at the top of the rabbit so you can hang it up. Or run a piece of yarn through the hole so that you can wear a rabbit around your neck.

4. To make the three-dimensional rabbit here, take a lump of clay, about half a cup, and begin to shape it as the illustration shows. Look at the front view and the side view. After studying them and playing with the "clay," you will be able to create a rabbit yourself.

5. **Ask an adult to help you turn on the oven.** Preheat it to 350°F. Cover a cookie sheet with aluminum foil and place the rabbit on it. If you are making more than one rabbit, place them all an inch apart, because the "clay" spreads as it bakes. Check after 10 minutes to make sure that the rabbit isn't burning around the edges. Bake for about 15 to 20 minutes, until the rabbit is just beginning to brown at the edges.

6. After the rabbit has cooled, paint it white. Allow it to dry and then draw the eyes, whiskers, and paws with the black fine-line marker. Mix a little red paint with the white paint to make pink for the nose and the inside of the ears. Paint them on the rabbit. ★

Eggshell Rabbits

These two eggshell rabbits will stand proud and tall in your Easter basket, or on your desk. They will look great when you put your decorated eggs around them and add some chocolate bunnies, chicks, and jellybeans.

HERE'S WHAT YOU WILL NEED★

2 raw eggs, 2 cotton balls
scrap of white felt
black fine-line marker
scissors, white glue, stapler, 2 strips of paper, $\frac{1}{2}''$ wide × 4″ long

HERE'S HOW TO DO IT★

1. Follow the directions for blowing out an egg on page 15.

2. Staple the ends of one strip of paper together to form a circle base for each egg. With the black marker, draw the rabbit's feet on each base, as shown in the illustration.

3. Draw the rabbit's face and front paws on the egg with the black marker. Glue the rabbit to the base. Glue a cotton ball on for a tail. Cut out ears from the white felt and glue them in place, checking the illustration. Repeat all the steps for the other rabbit. Now your rabbits are ready to be put in your Easter basket.★

Rebecca and Raymond Clothespin Rabbits

These wooden rabbits are made from two clothespins each. They can be made into a pin, strung on a necklace, or used to decorate an Easter basket.

HERE'S WHAT YOU WILL NEED★

4 plain wooden clothespins
2 cotton balls, glue
black fine-line marker
white and red acrylic paints, brush
¼" wide ribbon, 12" long
2 pipe cleaners, safety pin
ribbon, scraps of fabric, scissors

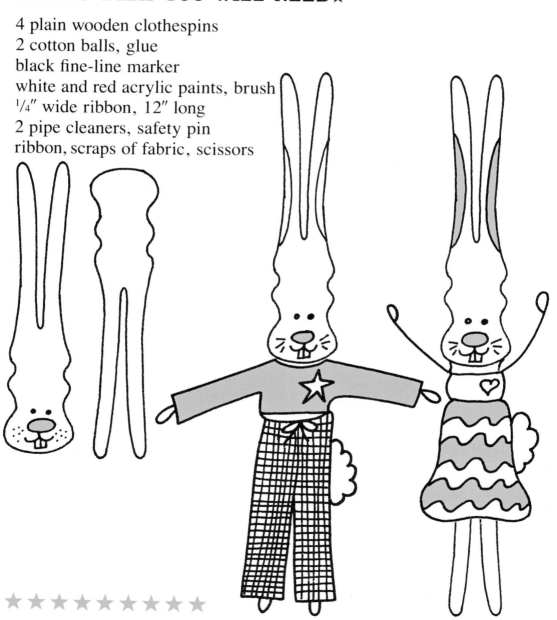

HERE'S HOW TO DO IT★

1. One clothespin will become the rabbit's head and ears. The other one will be the body and legs. Glue the end of one clothespin onto the end of the other, to form a rabbit like those shown in the illustration. Repeat this for the other rabbit.

2. Paint the rabbits white and then mix a little red paint with a small amount of white to make pink. Paint the inside of the ears and nose pink. Also paint a small heart on each, as shown.

3. With the black fine-line marker, draw on the faces for both rabbits, checking the illustration.

4. To make the arms, center the clothespin body on a pipe cleaner. Wrap the pipe cleaner around the rabbit's body. Secure in the back with some glue. Allow glue to dry. Bend each pipe-cleaner arm in half and twist the end to form a paw. Repeat for the other rabbit.

5. You can make your rabbits some simple clothes using the scraps of fabric. Cut out a skirt and pants and glue them onto the rabbits. You can cut out a dress by folding a rectangle of fabric in half. Then cut a hole for the head to go through and tie a strip of fabric around the waist for a belt. To make a shirt for the boy rabbit, follow the same method, but cut off the bottom part. Check the illustrations for ideas. Glue on a cotton ball to make a tail.

6. To make a pin with the rabbit, glue a safety pin onto the back of the rabbit. To make a necklace, take the ribbon and tie it around the rabbit's neck, knot it, and then knot the ends to secure it. When Rebecca and Raymond are finished, you can glue them to a container that you have already decorated or to a plain-colored box. The rabbits could also be placed inside your Easter basket. If you make several of them, you can give them away as presents. They could also be tied onto a present as a special treat. ★

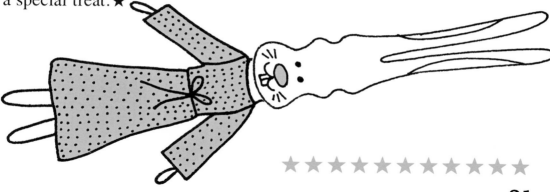

Bess and Brent Sock Rabbits

These country rabbits are cut out of a pair of white cotton socks. They are sewn, stuffed, and dressed. They are put together with a running stitch and their edges are left raggedy. Bess and Brent are two soft originals that would be a nice addition to your Easter decorations. Their overall size is about ten inches. You can make Bess, Brent, or both rabbits.

HERE'S WHAT YOU WILL NEED★

2 pairs of clean white cotton socks
   (1 pair for each rabbit)
scissors, needle, white thread
stuffing material (polyester pillow stuffing,
   old panty hose, cotton balls, or tissues)
black permanent marker
4 red buttons, for eyes
scrap of red felt, for hearts
scraps of colored fabric, for clothing
fancy button for front of shawl
beads for necklace

HERE'S HOW TO DO IT★

1. Follow the illustration on page 34 and cut the socks to form the head, body, ears, arms, and legs. Also check the illustration to see how to make the stitch you need. Cut out the various shapes. Trim each shape according to the dotted lines.

2. Begin by stuffing the head with your stuffing material and then wind a piece of thread around the neck. Tie it with a knot.

3. Stuff the body and then stitch the bottom edge closed. Sew up each leg, stuff, and then sew it onto the body, as shown in the illustration. Sew the arms, leaving the straight end open. Stuff and then attach to the body, as shown. Now sew up the ears, again leaving the straight end open. Stuff them and sew them on, as shown in the illustration.

4. Sew on the button eyes, and draw on a nose, mouth, and whiskers with the marker. Cut out a heart from the scrap of red felt, and then glue it in place.

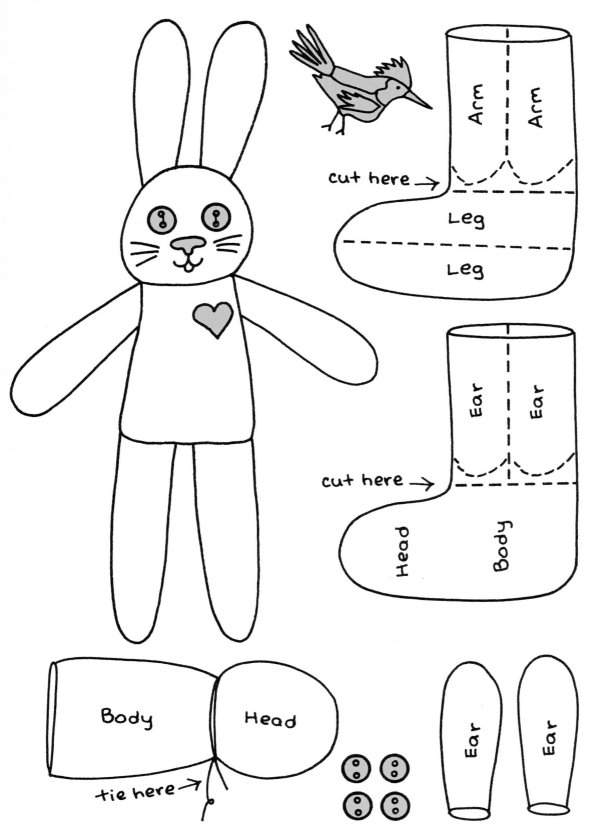

cut here →

Arm   Arm

Leg

Leg

cut here →

Ear   Ear

Head   Body

Body   Head

tie here →

Ear   Ear

5. To make clothes, decide if you are making Bess or Brent. For Bess, start by cutting out a 4″ × 12″ piece of fabric for her shawl and put it around her. Overlap the two edges in front and sew on a fancy button. To make the skirt, cut a 6″ × 12″ piece of fabric. Fold it in half and sew up the one side seam that is open. With the needle and a long piece of thread, make a running stitch about ¼″ from the top edge. Put the skirt on Bess and pull the thread gently around her body until it fits tightly. Tie a knot and then arrange the skirt.

6. To make pants for Brent, cut a 6″ × 10″ piece of fabric. Fold it in half and sew up the side seam. Checking the illustration, make a cut to form the legs. Sew up the slit. Place the pants on Brent. With a needle and a long piece of thread, make a running stitch about ¼″ from the top edge. Put the pants on Brent and pull the thread gently around his body until it fits tightly. Tie with a knot. ★

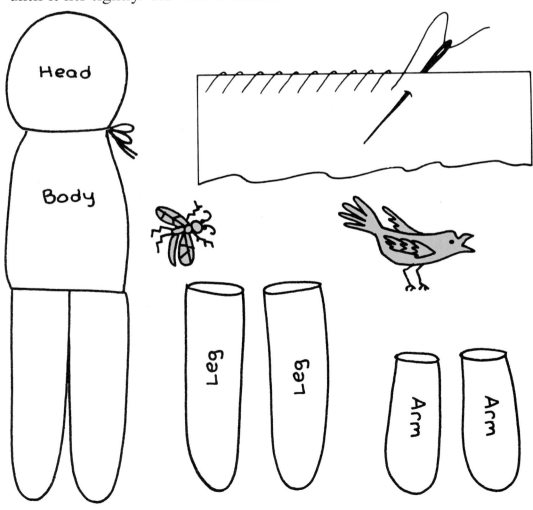

Easter Egg Tree

The Easter egg tree was invented in Europe over a hundred years ago and is still a lovely way to display Easter eggs. It makes a great centerpiece for an Easter celebration. Use it to show off your beautifully decorated eggs.

HERE'S WHAT YOU WILL NEED★

several tree branches, each about 2 feet long, with small twigs
an empty pound coffee can
plaster of Paris, water, measuring cups, or a small container of
  premixed plaster compound
green construction paper, glue, string, ruler
decorated Easter eggs that have been blown out and cleaned
ribbon

HERE'S HOW TO DO IT★

1. Follow the directions on the package of plaster of Paris and make about two cups of it. Fill the coffee can with the mixture. If you are using the premixed compound, just empty it into the coffee can.

2. Place the ends of the branches directly into the plaster. Use a piece of string to tie them together at the bottom, just above the plaster, to keep them secure. Allow them to dry in place. Cover the coffee can with a piece of green construction paper. You can glue it onto the can. Tie a piece of ribbon around the can and make a bow to decorate it.

3. For each egg that you plan to hang on your Easter egg tree, cut a 6″ piece of string. Fold the string in half, and knot it. Glue the knot to the top of the egg. Allow to dry. Repeat this for all the eggs. Hang each egg on a twig.★

Regina and Reginald Rabbit

Regina and Reginald are fun to create out of fabric and decorate with paints. What wonderful Easter presents they would make for someone special.

HERE'S WHAT YOU WILL NEED★

¹/₂ yard of muslin fabric (will make at least 4 rabbits)
stuffing material (polyester, old pantyhose, cotton balls, tissues)
white sewing thread
straight pins
needle, thread, scissors
pencil
black fine-line marker
tracing paper, carbon paper
several small brushes
several colors of acrylic paint

Note: If your mom has a sewing machine, she could help you to sew them.

HERE'S HOW TO DO IT★

1. Make patterns for Regina and Reginald by tracing the pictures here and cutting them out.

2. Take the muslin and fold it in half. Pin the pattern onto the muslin and trace around the outline with a pencil. Leave the pins in and cut out the pattern about ¹/₄″ outside the pattern line. Remove the pattern and the pins. This will make one rabbit.

3. Sew the two pieces together along the pattern line, leaving a 1¹/₂″ opening for the stuffing to go through.

4. Carefully trim the material near the curves so that the finished rabbit won't pucker. Turn the rabbit inside out so the rough edges are hidden. Fill with the stuffing and then stitch up the opening.

5. Draw on the rabbit's features and the outlines of its clothes with the black marker. Then, with the acrylic paints, color them in. Repeat for the other rabbit. ★

Easter Morning Pancake

This is a delicious pancake that has confectioners' sugar sprinkled on top and is served with strawberry jam. One pancake, cut in half, serves two people. The recipe here makes two pancakes and will serve four people.

INGREDIENTS:

1 cup flour
1 cup milk
4 eggs
1 teaspoon cinnamon
8 tablespoons sweet butter,
  divided in half
confectioners' sugar
strawberry jam

UTENSILS:

measuring cups and spoons
mixing bowl and spoon
two 8″ round baking pans
potholder, sifter

HERE'S HOW TO DO IT★

1. **Ask an adult to help you with the cooking.** Turn on the oven and preheat to 400°.

2. Combine the flour, milk, eggs, and cinnamon in the mixing bowl.

3. Place a baking pan with 4 tablespoons of butter in it on top of a stove burner. Turn the burner on to medium-low heat and let the butter melt and begin to bubble. Add half of the batter. Repeat for the other pan and then place both pans in the oven. Bake for about 15 to 20 minutes, or until the edges of the pancakes begin to brown. Using potholders, remove from the oven. Sift some confectioners' sugar over each pancake. Serve with about 2 tablespoons of strawberry jam. ★

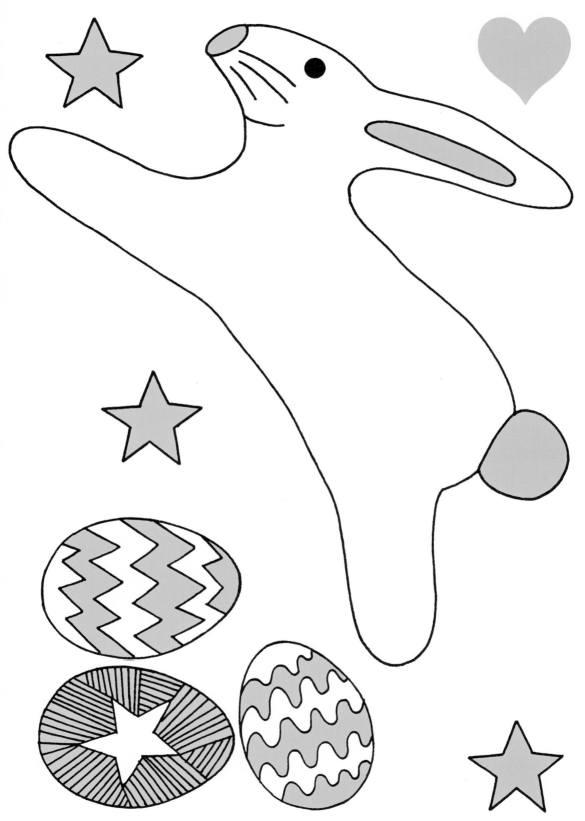

Bunny Cookies

These delicious gingerbread bunny cookies are so good that they may not make it into your Easter basket. The cookies can have raisin eyes or you can make them really fancy by using sugar icing to "draw" on them.

INGREDIENTS ★

3/4 cup firmly packed dark brown sugar
1/2 cup butter, softened
2 eggs
1/4 cup molasses
3 1/4 cups flour
2 teaspoons ginger
1 1/2 teaspoons baking soda
1 teaspoon cinnamon
1/2 teaspoon nutmeg
1/2 teaspoon salt
24 raisins
3/4 cup, plus 1 tablespoon confectioners' sugar
1 tablespoon milk
food coloring—red for nose and eyes, yellow
    for tail, and blue for the ribbon
extra flour, for rolling out the cookie dough

UTENSILS ★

measuring cups and spoons
large mixing bowl, mixing spoon
aluminum foil
rolling pin
cardboard, tracing paper, pencil, scissors
2 cookie sheets, covered with aluminum foil
knife, potholder
small mixing bowl, spoon
3 cups, 3 toothpicks

HERE'S HOW TO DO IT★

1. **Ask an adult to help you turn on the oven.** Preheat it to 350°.

2. In the large mixing bowl, beat the sugar and butter until well blended. Add the eggs and molasses and stir until the ingredients are completely combined. Stir in the flour, ginger, baking soda, cinnamon, nutmeg, and salt. Cover the bowl with the aluminum foil and place in the refrigerator for an hour.

3. Roll the dough to ⅛″ thickness on a lightly floured surface.

4. To make the pattern for the bunny cookie, place the tracing paper over the bunny design and draw over it with a pencil. Turn the paper over and rub along the lines of the pattern on the back with the pencil. Turn the paper over again and place it on the piece of cardboard. Draw over the original line with the pencil and then cut it out.

5. Place the cardboard pattern on the rolled-out dough and cut around the outside edges with a knife. Lift the pattern and repeat.

6. After the cookies have been cut out, place them 1″ apart on the cookie sheets. Use raisins to make the eyes for each bunny, or draw them on with colored icing after the cookies have been baked.

7. Bake the cookies for 10 minutes. Remove from the cookie sheets after they have cooled for 15 minutes and place on a platter for serving.

8. If you want to decorate the cookies with colored icing, combine the confectioners' sugar with the milk in the small bowl. Divide the mixture evenly into the three cups. Add a drop of food coloring to each cup—red, yellow, and blue. Stir each cup. Using the toothpick as a pencil, draw eyes, nose, and ribbon on the bunnies. Enjoy!★

Chocolate-swirl Fudge

Chocolate and marshmallows combine in a swirl to make this great fudge. It is sure to please everyone. Several pieces wrapped in clear plastic and tied with a brightly colored ribbon make a good Easter present.

INGREDIENTS ★

3 cups of semisweet chocolate pieces
4 tablespoons butter, divided in half
1 can sweetened condensed milk
2 teaspoons vanilla
pinch of salt
2 cups of miniature marshmallows

UTENSILS ★

8″ square pan
measuring cups and spoons
mixing spoon
large saucepan
medium-sized saucepan
knife
clear plastic wrap
ribbon

HERE'S HOW TO DO IT★

1. Line an 8″ square pan with aluminum foil and set aside.

2. **Ask an adult to help you with the cooking.** In the large saucepan, melt the chocolate chips with 2 tablespoons of the butter, the condensed milk, vanilla, and salt. Stir until completely combined.

3. Remove the saucepan from the heat and spread the mixture evenly in the prepared pan.

4. In the medium-sized saucepan, over low heat, melt the marshmallows with the remaining 2 tablespoons of butter. Spread this over the fudge. Then take a knife and make swirls through the fudge to give it an interesting pattern.

5. Refrigerate the fudge for about 2 hours, or until firm. Remove from the pan and peel off the aluminum foil. If you cut the fudge into 1″ squares, you will have 64 pieces. ★

Acorn Cookies

At Easter time the squirrels feast on the stash of acorns that they have collected and stored. I'm not sure that they would like these acorn-shaped butter cookies, but you will.

INGREDIENTS★

1 cup sweet butter, softened
3/4 cup brown sugar, firmly packed
3 egg yolks
2 3/4 cups all-purpose flour
1/2 cup finely chopped pecans
1 teaspoon vanilla
1/2 teaspoon baking powder
1/2 pounds caramel candies
1/4 cup water
1 cup chocolate sprinkles

UTENSILS★

measuring cups and spoons
large mixing bowl
mixing spoon
mixing fork
cookie sheets covered with aluminum foil
pot holders
small saucepan
dinner plate
waxed paper

HERE'S HOW TO DO IT★

1. **Ask an adult to help you to turn on the oven and to use the stove.** Preheat the oven to 350°. Wash your hands before you begin.

2. In the large mixing bowl, beat together the butter, sugar, and egg yolks until they are smooth and fluffy. Now stir in the flour, chopped pecans, vanilla, and baking powder. Stir this mixture until it is well blended.

3. To make each cookie, use your hands to shape a heaping teaspoon of dough into a ball. With your fingers, gently pinch the dough to form a round point at the top, and shape the dough ball to look like an acorn, as shown in the illustration. Place the acorn cookies point side up, about 1″ apart on the baking sheets. Bake for 12 minutes, or until slightly browned.

4. Put the caramels and the water in the small saucepan, over low heat. Stir the mixture until the caramels are melted and combined with the water. Remove from the heat.

5. Pour the chocolate sprinkles onto the dinner plate. Dip the large end of each cookie into the caramel and then into the chocolate sprinkles. Place the cookies on waxed paper until the caramel hardens. Makes about 6 dozen cookies.★

Index